BUNNY
WILL NOT
SMILE!

HELP!

WRITTEN AND ILLUSTRATED
BY JASON THARP

Ready-to-Read

Simon Spotlight
New York   London   Toronto   Sydney   New Delhi

SIMON SPOTLIGHT

An imprint of Simon & Schuster Children's Publishing Division

1230 Avenue of the Americas, New York, New York 10020

This Simon Spotlight edition December 2018

Text and illustrations copyright © 2018 by Jason Tharp

For information about special discounts for bulk purchases, please contact Simon & Schuster Special Sales at 1-866-506-1949 or business@simonandschuster.com.

Manufactured in the United States of America 1118 LAK

10 9 8 7 6 5 4 3 2 1

This book has been cataloged with the Library of Congress.

ISBN 978-1-5344-2509-5 (hc)

ISBN 978-1-5344-2508-8 (pbk)

ISBN 978-1-5344-2510-1 (eBook)

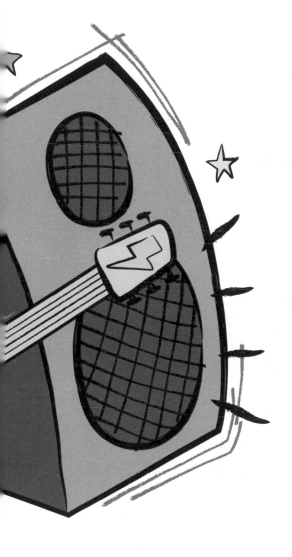

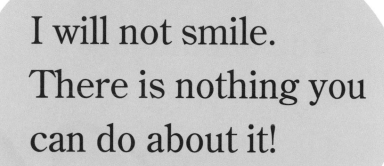

I will not smile.
There is nothing you
can do about it!

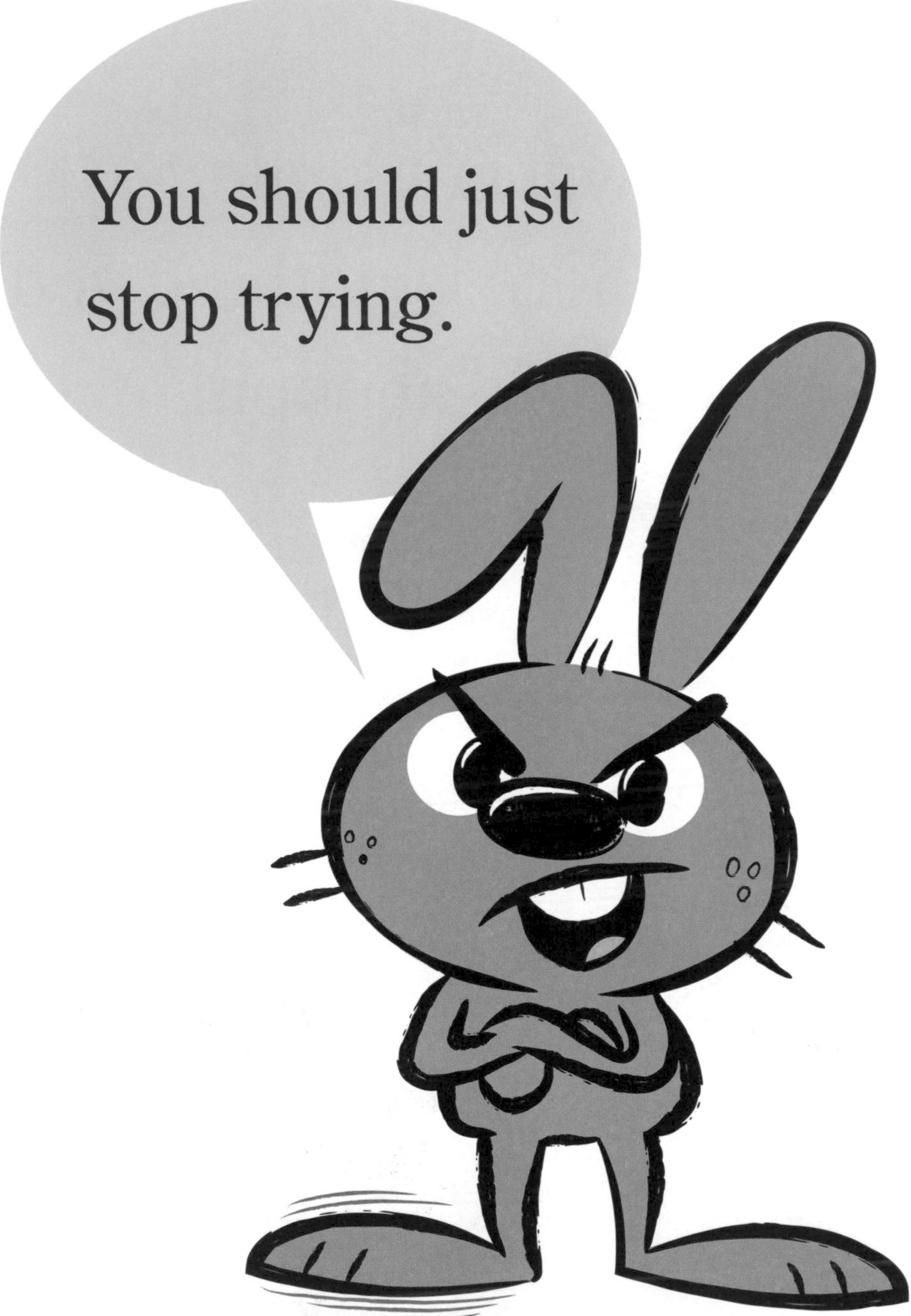
You should just stop trying.

Next time we see Bunny,
I need you to make
a super silly face!

One.

Two.

Three.

Now!

Stop it!
I cannot stop smiling!
You are way too
silly and funny.